Little Whistle

Cynthia Rylant

Illustrated by Tim Bowers

Harcourt, Inc.

San Diego   New York   London

To Samantha and Bain Wills
—C.R.

To all our new friends in Granville
—T. B.

visit us at www.abdopublishing.com

Reinforced library bound edition published in 2007 by Spotlight, a division of ABDO Publishing Group, Edina, Minnesota. This edition was published by agreement with Harcourt, Inc. www.harcourt.com

Text copyright © 2001 by Cynthia Rylant
Illustrations copyright © 2001 by Tim Bowers

Library of Congress Cataloging-in-Publication Data

Rylant, Cynthia.
   Little Whistle / Cynthia Rylant ; illustrated by Tim Bowers.
      p. cm.
   Summary: At night after the shades are drawn, a small guinea pig shares adventures with the toys in Toytown, the toy store where he lives.
   ISBN-13: 978-1-59961-253-9 (reinforced library bound edition)
   ISBN-10: 1-59961-253-4 (reinforced library bound edition)
   [1. Guinea pigs--Fiction. 2. Toys--Fiction.]   I. Bowers, Tim, ill. II. Title.

PZ7.R982Lh 2007
[E]--dc22

2006030170

All Spotlight books have reinforced library bindings
and are manufactured in the United States of America.

Little Whistle was the only live thing in Toytown. He lived in a small cage at the back of the store. He was furry and brown, and all of the children who came to look at toys most loved looking at him. But Little Whistle was always sleeping, so he did not look back.

Each night when Toytown closed and the shades were drawn and all the children gone, Little Whistle woke up. Then he climbed out of his cage, put on his blue pea coat, and began a new adventure.

Some adventures were quiet—as when he found a lovely book about bears to read. And some adventures were loud—as when he discovered the trumpet. But whenever Little Whistle was awake, *something* was going on.

Little Whistle's blue pea coat had been given to him his first night in Toytown. The store owner did not know that guinea pigs can become quite chilly, and she had not put enough bedding in Little Whistle's cage. The small guinea pig was all alone and shivering when he heard someone say, "Here, lad, warm your bones with me coat."

Little Whistle looked up and saw a wooden sailor waving to him from a big boat on a shelf! Little Whistle had not known toys could talk. But he was too chilly to be afraid, so he climbed from his cage and put on the sailor's warm coat. Little Whistle talked with the sailor all night long, about the sea and fog and gulls and full moons over the waves.

When morning came and it was nearly time for the shades to go up and the store to open, Little Whistle went back to his cage. He tucked the pea coat inside a hollow log, for the sailor said he might keep it awhile. Then he went to sleep.

That day the sailor went home with a happy boy, taking his boat but leaving the blue pea coat behind. Little Whistle planned to return the coat as soon as he saw the sailor again. In the meantime, it made a very dashing wardrobe!

Little Whistle had many good friends in Toytown. There was Lion, who loved vanilla cookies. (One day a little girl had given him one, and since then he had talked of nothing else.) There was Rabbit, who always wanted to run. (And when the store was closed, she *did*.) There was Bear, who liked hats; Violet, a little china doll who sang; and many more, depending on who had been sold, of course.

None of the toys were real, but this did not mean the toys could not eat vanilla cookies or run or sing or like hats. Most toys will do these things, once the shades are drawn.

Each night Little Whistle visited all of his friends. If the store was especially chilly, he borrowed a hat from Bear. The store was quite large, so some nights Little Whistle took the train from one end to the other. And some nights he just walked.

There was always a tea party going on somewhere. Or a game of checkers.

Babies were being read to. (Soldier especially liked to read, and sometimes had several babies all around him.)

Toytown was the sweetest and kindest place in the world for a small guinea pig to live. Little Whistle loved the store and his friends. And he did not mind when someone was sold. Toys love being sold to children who care for them. Little Whistle knew this and understood.

But he also knew that he would never be sold, and
this pleased him, for he felt there was no better
home in the world for him than Toytown. With
quiet contentment, Little Whistle tucked the warm
blue pea coat inside his log each morning and curled
into sleep, waiting for the night . . .

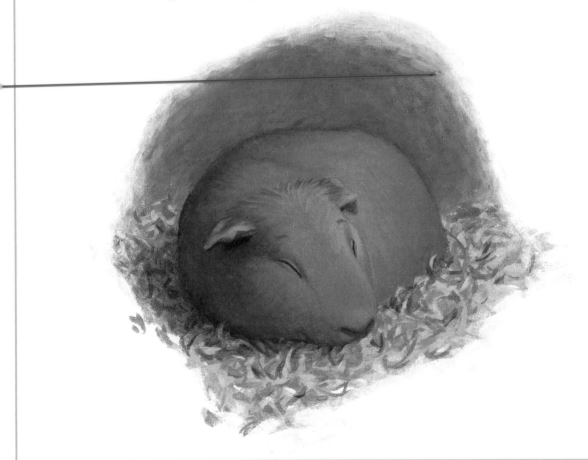

waiting for the shades to be drawn.